To d
(who is always on the go)
because turkeys are smart
— G.M.

For P. D. Eastman
— J.M.

Text copyright © 2010 by Grace Maccarone
Illustrations copyright © 2010 by John Manders

All rights reserved. Published by Scholastic Inc.
SCHOLASTIC, CARTWHEEL BOOKS, and associated logos
are trademarks and/or registered trademarks of Scholastic Inc.
Lexile is a registered trademark of MetaMetrics, Inc.

Library of Congress Cataloging-in-Publication Data is available.

ISBN 978-0-545-12001-2

10 9 8 7 6 5 4   14 15

Printed in the U.S.A. 40
First printing, September 2010

Turkey Day

SCHOLASTIC READER
LEVEL 1
50-250 WORDS

by Grace Maccarone
illustrated by John Manders

Cartwheel
·B·O·O·K·S·®

SCHOLASTIC INC.
New York   Toronto   London   Auckland
Sydney   Mexico City   New Delhi   Hong Kong

Wake up, turkeys!
Don't be slow.
It is time to
go, go, go!

Turkeys go
from near and far.

They go by bike.
They go by car.

They go by bus.

They go by train.

They go by boat.
They go by plane.

Marching turkeys
walk in rows.

Dancers leap
on tippy-toes.

**Turkeys flap
and flop . . .**

. . . and flip!

Turkeys trot . . .

. . . and trip and skip.

Turkeys meet.

Turkeys greet.

Turkeys all
sit down to eat.

The turkeys sing
and dance and play.

What a happy
TURKEY DAY!